To Emily and Michelle,

   We will miss you at Blessed Kateri School. We will think of you in warm, sunny Florida. Hope you enjoy your new school and new home.

   Love
   Your Friends at Blessed Kateri
   in Kitchener, Ontario.

Hazel's Circle

Story by Sharon Phillips Denslow

Pictures by Sharon McGinley-Nally

Maxwell Macmillan Canada Toronto

Maxwell Macmillan International
New York Oxford Singapore Sydney

Four Winds Press
New York

Four Winds Press, Macmillan Publishing Company, 866 Third Avenue, New York, NY 10022.
Maxwell Macmillan Canada, Inc., 1200 Eglinton Avenue East, Suite 200, Don Mills, Ontario
M3C 3N1. Macmillan Publishing Company is part of the Maxwell Communication Group of
Companies. First American edition. Printed and bound in Hong Kong by South China Printing Company
(1988) Ltd. 10 9 8 7 6 5 4 3 2 1 The text of this book is set in Souvenir Gothic
Library of Congress Cataloging-in-Publication Data. Denslow, Sharon Phillips.   Hazel's circle / by
Sharon Phillips Denslow ; pictures by Sharon McGinley-Nally.   p.   cm.   Summary: Hazel finds that taking
her pet rooster Ike along on her rounds to sell eggs to her neighbors creates a number of exciting adventures.
ISBN 0-02-728683-5. [1. Roosters—Fiction. 2. Neighborliness—Fiction.] I. McGinley-Nally, Sharon, ill. II.
Title. PZ7.D433 Haz 1992 [E]—dc20 91-18182

A NOTE FROM THE ARTIST

The illustrations in this book were primarily painted with Rotring Artists Colors (a liquid watercolor that produces very vivid colors), inks, watercolors, and acrylics. I use 140-lb. Arches
cold press 100%-rag watercolor paper, and I usually draw the images first and add color
and designs as I proceed. The finished paintings were color-separated using
four-color process. A special thanks to Julie Quan.

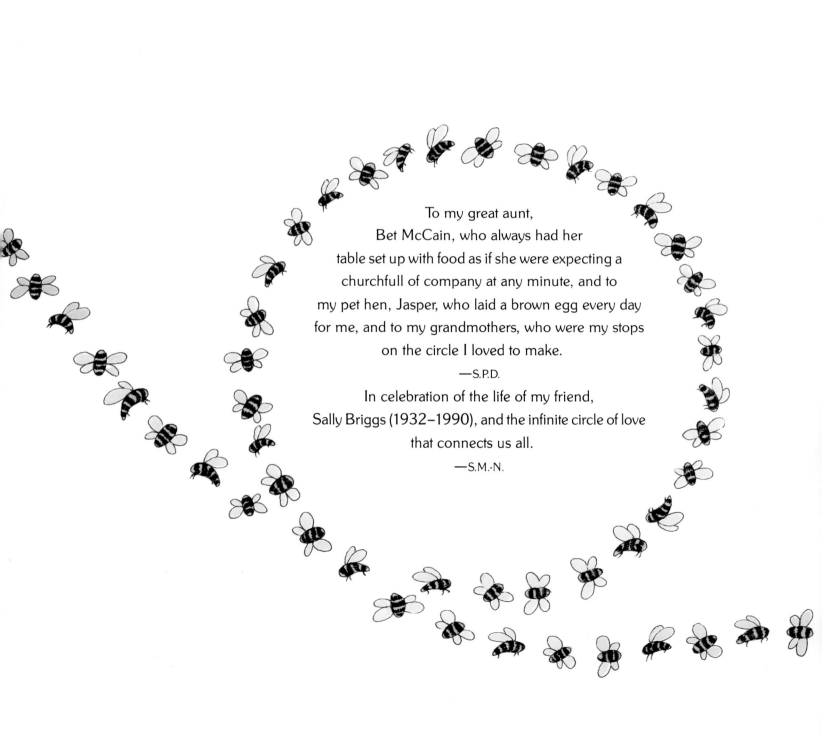

To my great aunt,
Bet McCain, who always had her
table set up with food as if she were expecting a
churchfull of company at any minute, and to
my pet hen, Jasper, who laid a brown egg every day
for me, and to my grandmothers, who were my stops
on the circle I loved to make.
—S.P.D.
In celebration of the life of my friend,
Sally Briggs (1932–1990), and the infinite circle of love
that connects us all.
—S.M.-N.

"Come on, Ike," Hazel says to her pet rooster, "I'm ready to make my circle."

Ike stops in the middle of his dust bath and considers Hazel's invitation. Then he starts flipping dust again.

"Okay," Hazel says, tying her money pouch around her waist. "I'll go myself."

Hazel picks up her egg basket and sets off down the path to her first customer's house.

Halfway there, she hears Ike running to catch her.

"You'll have to keep up," she warns him, "and don't get into trouble this time."

But Ike has already spotted Pete, Rae Allen's big gray cat. Ike makes a dash for Pete, chasing him all the way across the field right up to Rae Allen's porch.

Rae Allen is an artist. Her house is painted bright blue with red trim. Sunflowers taller than Hazel are painted on the side of her barn. Rae Allen also paints rocks and earrings and gourds and straw hats and Hazel's toenails every time she visits.

"Hi, Hazel," Rae Allen calls. "Come in and see what I made yesterday."

Hazel steps into the shadowy kitchen.

"Everything's purple!" she exclaims. Rows and rows of homemade grape juice reflect their cool, amethyst color across the floor and walls and ceiling, and across Hazel and Rae Allen and Pete.

"Try some," Rae Allen says, handing Hazel a glass of juice, "and then let's get to those toenails!"

"It even tastes purple," Hazel says with a purple-lipped grin.

After their visit, Hazel gives Rae Allen her six eggs for a quarter. Then Rae Allen puts three pint-jars of grape juice into a basket, wedging newspapers between the jars to keep them from clinking.

"One for Bet and Clyde, one for Roger, and one for you to take home," she says.

Ike sidles up beside Rae Allen's orange and yellow toenails and takes a quick peck.

"Ouch, shoo away!"

"Ike!" Hazel yells. "I guess he thought your toenails were corn."

"You better watch out," Rae Allen says to Ike. "I'll paint *your* toes next time."

Bet and Clyde's house is across the creek. Hazel wades
through the one remaining spring-fed water hole,
sandals, fuchsia toenails, and all, sending water striders
and pale-colored crawfish scooting to safety under a
soapstone ledge.

Ike runs up and down beside the thin stream of water,
not wanting to get wet.

"You won't melt," Hazel says, "and Bet and Clyde are
waiting."

Finally the big rooster flaps his wings, splashes across
the creek, and sprints up the bank, ruffling his feathers.

"Nice color today," greets Bet, peering at Hazel's toenails.

"Thank you," says Hazel.

"How are your hens taking this heat?" asks Clyde.

"Still laying," Hazel says proudly, and she gives Bet and Clyde their six eggs for a quarter.

"Oh, there he goes again!" Hazel warns as Ike heads toward the picnic table.

But Ike knows where he's welcome. At Bet and Clyde's, Ike is considered company, too.

"He's got better manners than most people," says Clyde, crumbling up a piece of corn bread for Ike.

"We had another visitor this morning. I thought you could take him home for us," Clyde says, smiling.

He removes a brick from the top of a cardboard box and flips the box over. A big striped garter snake uncoils himself and flicks his tongue in and out.

"Pipestem!" Hazel says, recognizing Roger's snake.

Bet sniffs, "I wish that boy would keep his snake at home."

Clyde and Hazel coil Pipestem around the jars of grape juice, and Bet tucks two fried pies in with the eggs.

"One for Roger and one for you," she says.

Hazel waves good-bye and continues on her circle,
taking a shortcut across the old Cole cemetery to
Roger's house. A bullfrog bells out his deep call from
the pond behind.

"Hello to you, too," Hazel calls back.

Ike trails cautiously behind, his eye on the snake basket.

"Ike," Hazel says, "quit being such a chicken!"

Hazel delivers six eggs to Roger's mother, and then, tucking the third quarter into her money pouch, she heads out to the backyard.

Roger's yard is so crowded with his experiments and seed jars and gauges and thermometers and sundials and birdhouses that it takes a minute for Hazel to spot Roger standing by his sister's wading pool.

"Guess who was visiting Bet and Clyde again?" she calls.

"I wondered where he was," Roger says, taking Pipestem out of the basket. "Did you see True Bart? We may set a record today. It's already up to ninety-six degrees."

Hazel stands on tiptoe to read the big yellow-and-black thermometer Roger has mounted on a post oak pole.

"Come on, Hazel," says Roger. "Come help me rescue these bees!"

Bees are all over the pool, crawling down the smooth
sides to the water, where most of them manage to fall in.

Roger hands Hazel a minnow net. "Clyde says they splash
water on themselves and go back to the hive and fan their
damp wings to help cool the hive down, but sometimes they
get too wet and heavy and fall into the water instead."

Hazel and Roger share Roger's pie and grape juice,
and rescue bees until True Bart climbs to ninety-eight.

The heat finally brings Ike to the edge of the pool for a drink.

"Hey, Ike, those aren't for you!" Roger shouts as the big rooster eyes the bees.

"Time to go home," Hazel says.

The trip across the cornfield back to Hazel's house is hot
and dusty.

Suddenly Ike stops and cranes his neck up and down
and from side to side at something between the rows
of corn.

"What do you see?" Hazel asks, carefully moving aside
some leaves and vines.

Ike does a quick step to one side and makes a funny hop.

Hazel looks again and laughs. "It's only a beetle."

Ike cocks his head at the beetle.

"Okay," Hazel says, "a very *big* beetle."

The beetle's feet scratch Hazel's hand as she admires its two long pincers and shining wings. Carefully she puts it in her egg basket. "Come on, Ike, let's go home and cool off."

Ike hears the hens in the yard and runs ahead. By the time Hazel reaches the house, he's in the middle of a wild dust bath.

Hazel goes to the faucet. Taking the hose, she shoots the water up in the air so that it makes a rainbow as it arcs back down on her head. A few drops fall on Ike, and he squawks in protest.

Hazel laughs at the fat, dusty rooster and settles down with
her baskets in the shade of the pear tree.

She admires her quarters, Bet's pie, the sparkling purple
grape juice, the big beetle, and her fuchsia toenails.

"We had a good circle today," she says to Ike, who has
come over in ruffled, dust-tipped feathers to claim his share
of the pie.